Such Fond Memories

—

A Mixed-Media Love Story

Tristan Tuttle

Southern Scribe Society

BALL GROUND, GEORGIA

Southern Scribe Society

Such Fond Memories

Southern Scribe Society
Ball Ground, GA 30107
www.southernscribesociety.com

Publisher's Note: This is a work of fiction. Names, characters, places, and incidents are a product of the author's imagination. Any resemblance to actual people, living or dead, or to businesses, companies, events, institutions, or locales is completely coincidental.

Book Layout © 2017 BookDesignTemplates.com
Cover Design by Abby Harding
Such Fond Memories/ Tristan Tuttle -- 1st ed.
ISBN 979-8-9998853-0-2

To Jared.
Ours is a love song for the long haul.

Author's Note

Dear Reader,

Such Fond Memories began as a procrastination project. Sorting out the mess I'd made of my first novel was too overwhelming of a task, so I, as I am oft prone to do, began avoiding it at all costs. Blackout poetry is essentially a word search that ends in a poem, and it became a great escape. (Shoutout to Austin Kleon whose book *Newspaper Blackout* introduced me to this art form.) Questioning my sanity while sorting through the hundreds of poems I created, I found a story begging to be told. The tale that revealed itself is as old as time: boy meets girl, they fall in love, fall apart, and then fall back together over the course of forty years.

The mixed-media element of *Such Fond Memories* makes this classic romance fresh and exciting. There's nothing better than a pair of scissors and a glue stick, and in an increasingly digital world, it's an act of defiance to create with your hands. As an analog artist, I can assure you that each story panel is hand-cut and pieced together with no digital assistance or manipulation of any kind. Most of the materials used in the creation of these collages were bound for the trash, which proves that art can be made from anything and by anyone as long as they're looking for it.

Just like the relationship in this book, what was once abandoned—each thrift store photo, old text book, outdated encyclopedia, or tiny speck of discarded ephemera—has new life in *Such Fond Memories*.

I hope that you enjoy *Such Fond Memories* as much as I enjoyed creating it over the past three years. For clarity and ease of reading, I've included the text beneath each image, and where necessary, I've added punctuation.

As of this writing, my novel is still a mess, but I am grateful for *this* story, the one I unexpectedly found hidden in old magazines and newspapers. I'll be finding little scraps of paper under bookcases and tables for years to come, a happy reminder of this accidental book.

May you find love (and art) everywhere you look!

Love,
Tristan

Contents

*"Climax," "Blissed," "Miracles," and "Beautifully Growing" were originally published as a set entitled *Bliss* in The Headlight Review's Vol.3 Num. 1

"Honor Her" was first published in Wildscape Lit's May 2025 Special Issue 1.

How did it all begin?
They had a good time together.
It changed his life.

I didn't think I'd fall in love.

I'm an unlikely candidate.

He was a good friend.

An amazing person.

Both have baggage for two.

We need balance.

This project was personal. She has spent her whole life searching for home.

Like a lynx pursuing a hare, he could scurry behind me in hot pursuit. The hunt has become the devotion and then—boom.

They spread a quilt near a tree.

They think of love.

All night they lay awake,

feeling.

Let's stay here a moment and savor the view.

I can't believe that we're looking at forever.

Clearly smitten by the intuitive husband,

"Lucky me!"

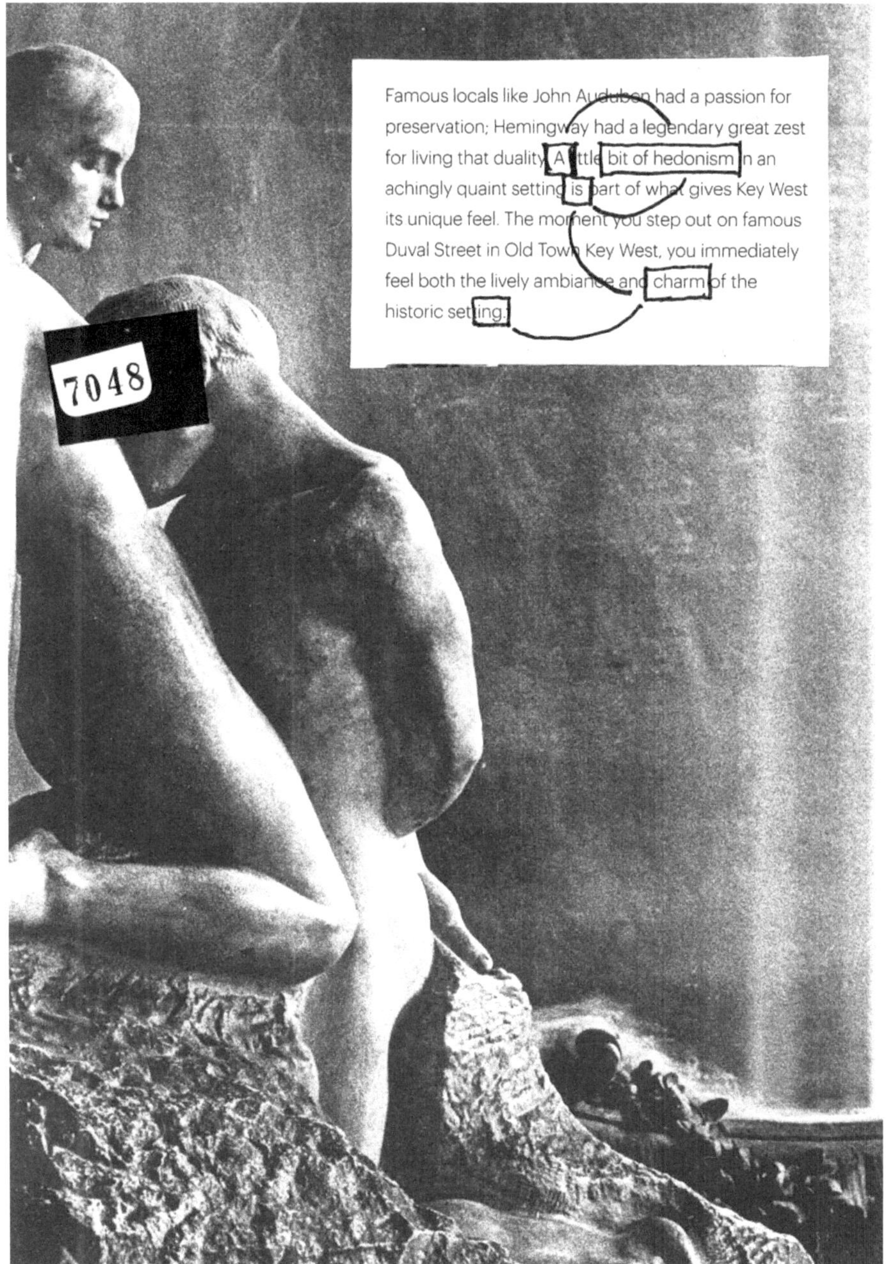

A bit of hedonism

is charming.

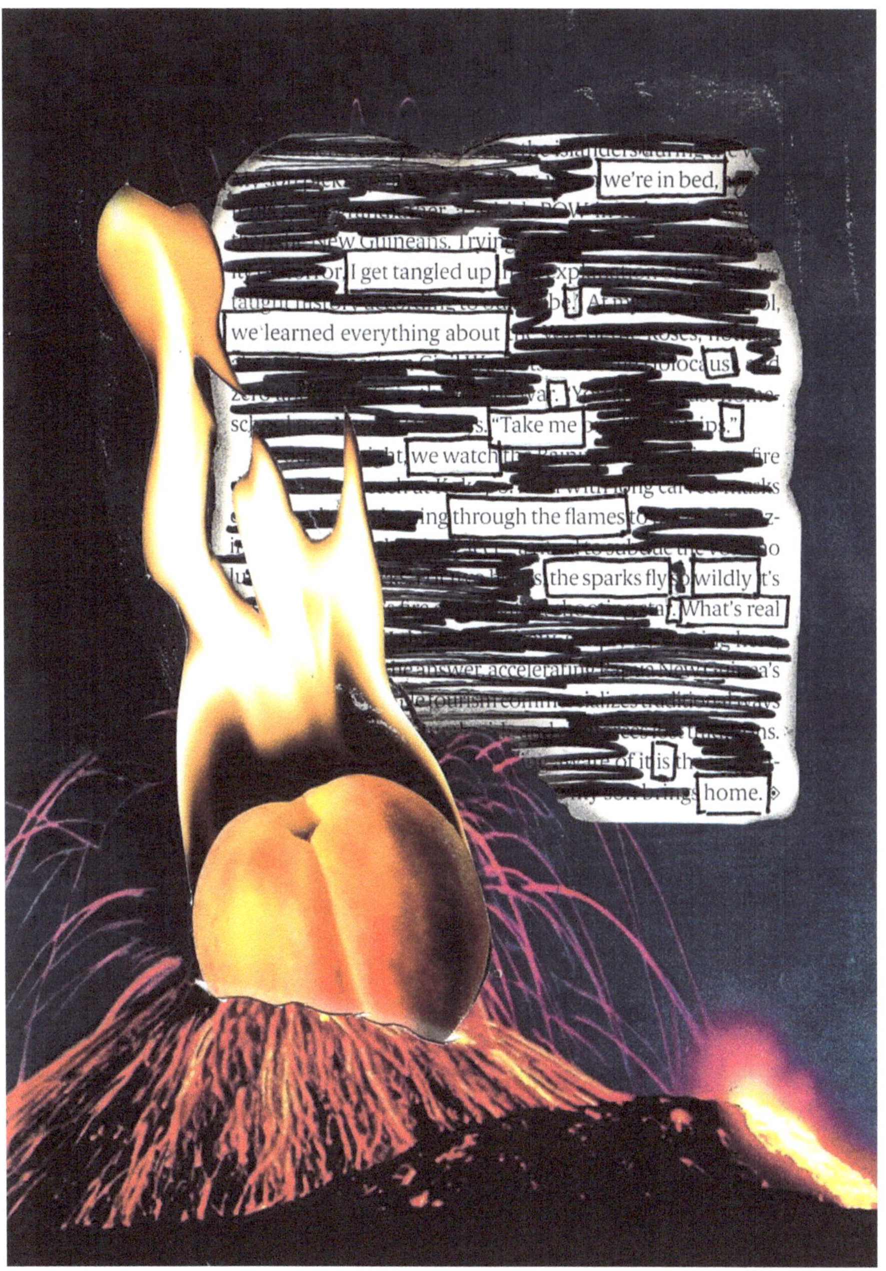

We're in bed. I get tangled up. We learned everything about us. "Take me." We watch through the flames the sparks fly wildly. What's real is home.

you returned the $20 bill for someone else to use.

Then we'd head for neighbor Bud Daughtry's little cinder-block vacation house near the ocean at Carolina Beach. I had no idea we lived on a peninsula called Federal Point (renamed Pleasure Island in 1972), with Bald Head Island to the south and Wrightsville Beach (a barrier island) to the north. All I knew was Carolina Beach, the Las Vegas of my Southern Baptist childhood: Ferris wheel, Putt-Putt golf, popcorn, Britt's Donut Shop.

And pier fishing.

In those vacation days of the '50s — Drewey's $20 bill in my father's wallet — I fished for many hours from the Carolina Beach pier, alongside loners, couples, and families. The choice for bait was bloodworms or shrimp. We were a bloodworm family. I remember one day when my line and hook dangled from the end of a yardstick. That pier birthed my hankering to fish, my love of the drama of hooking and pulling in supper.

Later in life, I fished inland ponds, usually with a Zebco spinning rod and black or red plastic or rubber worms to catch bass, or with a cane pole and Catawba worms to catch bream. In midlife, for a year in the fall from 1981 to 2001, fishing-age buddies and I traveled to Portsmouth

I had no idea pleasure was the choice that birthed my love of life.

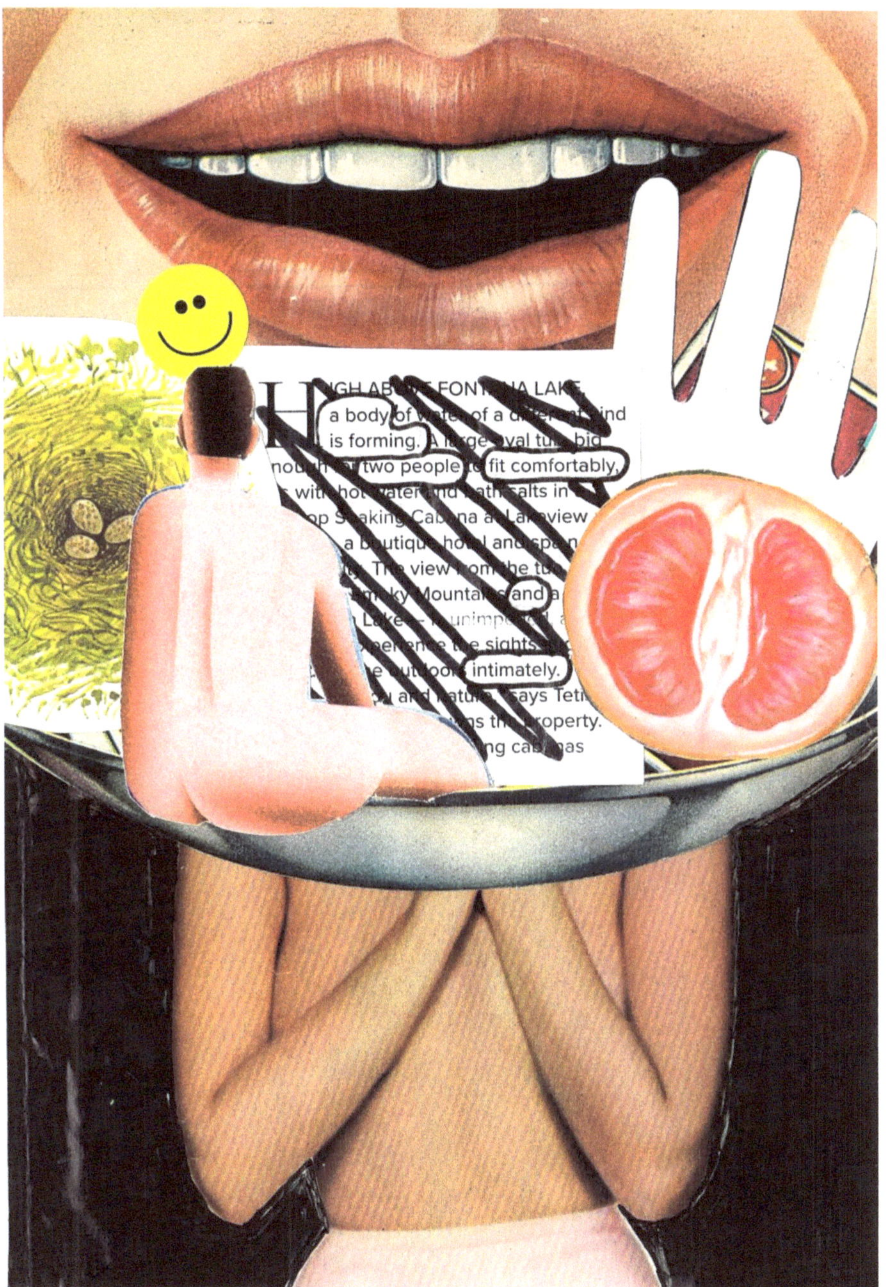

A body is forming.

Two people fit comfortably and intimately.

Climax came. I looked at God.

He said, "I'm going to give you all something great."

Too blissed out to care.

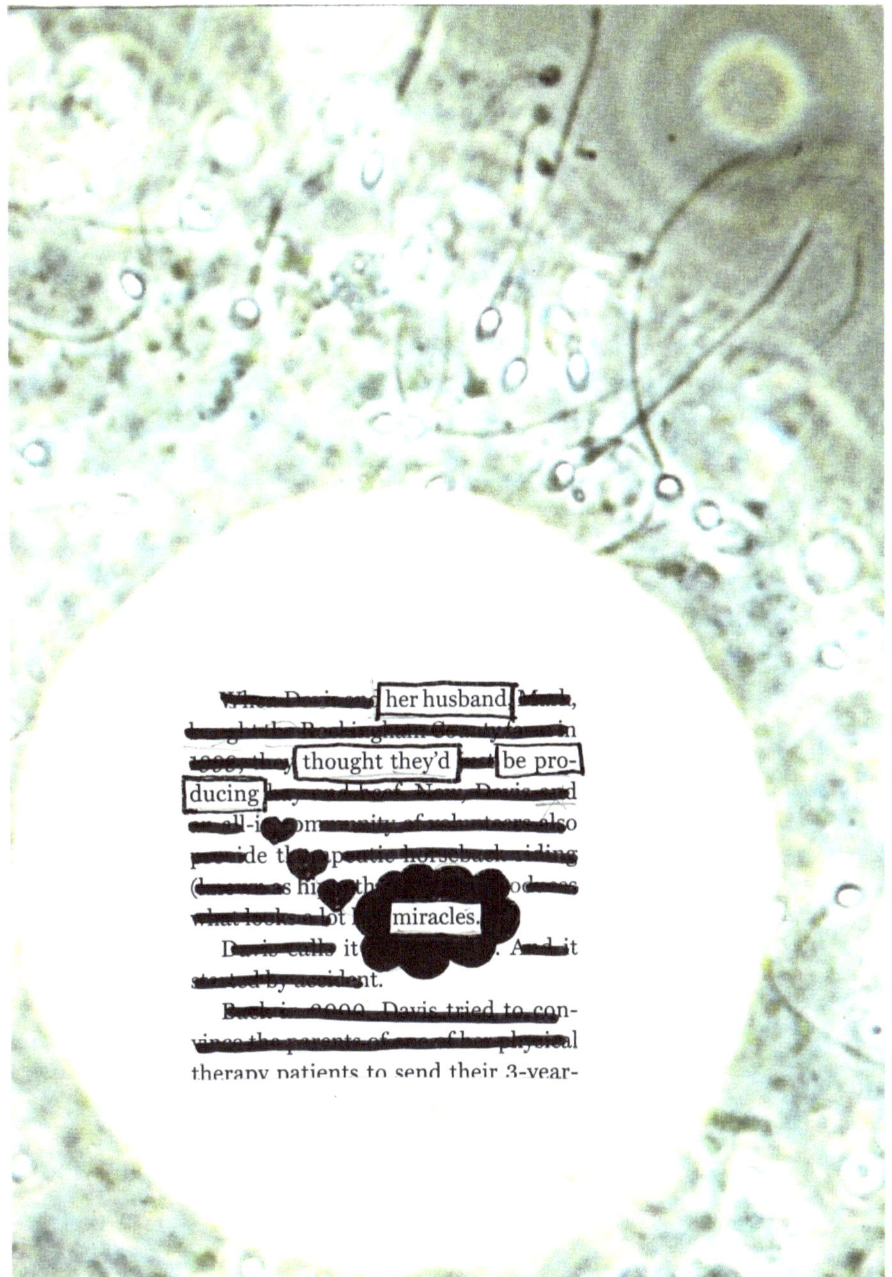

Her husband

thought they'd be producing miracles.

Beautifully

growing.

The home's character brought in everyday life. The details pass for art. A home is the sum of feeling where you want to be.

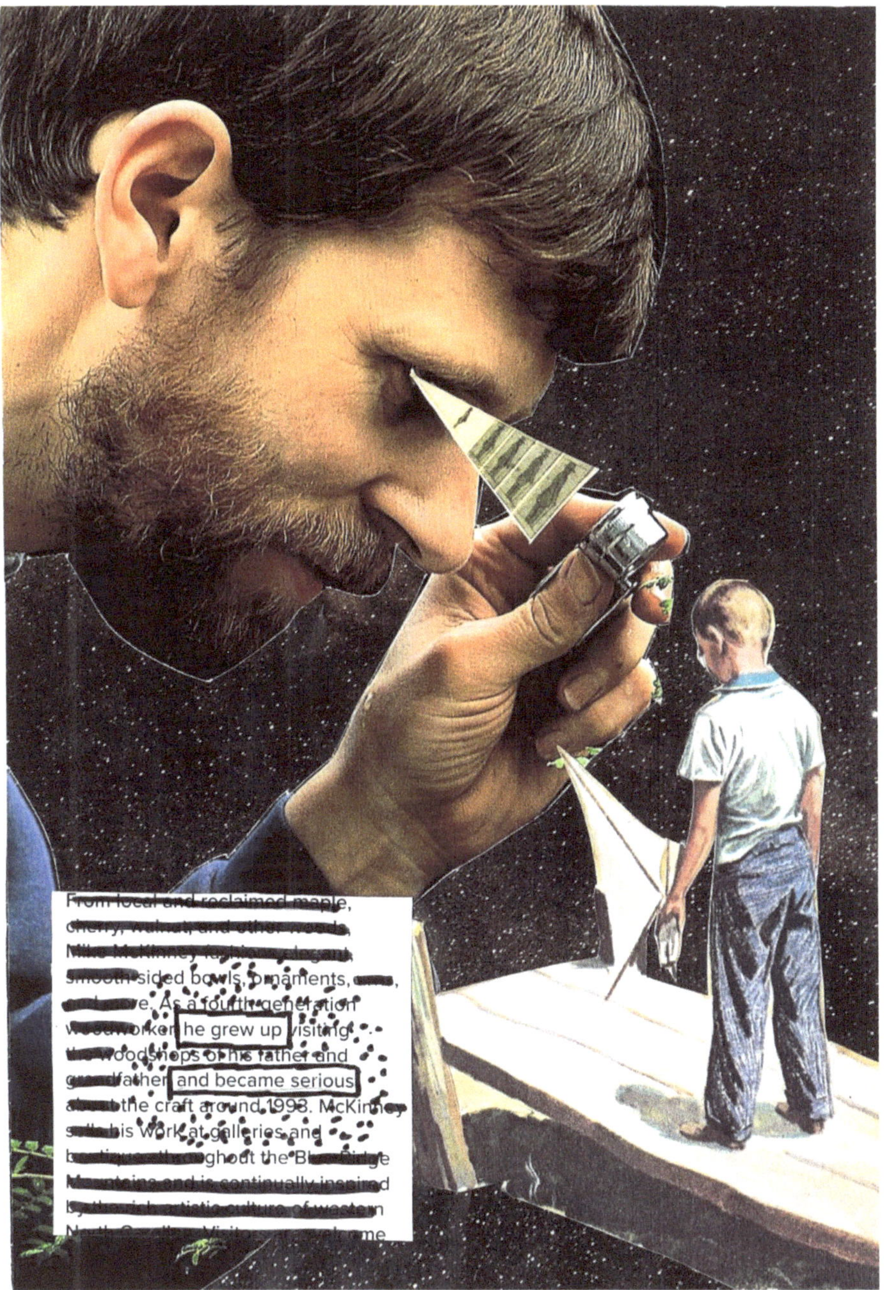

He grew up and became serious.

She carves her child,

a design and memory.

I love. You love. Someone loves you.

I gather our joy.

Their plan is to be genuine.

To follow and subvert time.

The child was beautiful and divine.

Mom's a light sleeper.

She just doesn't want me to get attacked by a bear.

The little girl took her first steps.

She started magic.

I stood before a family. Mine.

The holiday declares, "Haven't the kids had a wonderful time?"

The wonder will remain in the Christmas miracle.

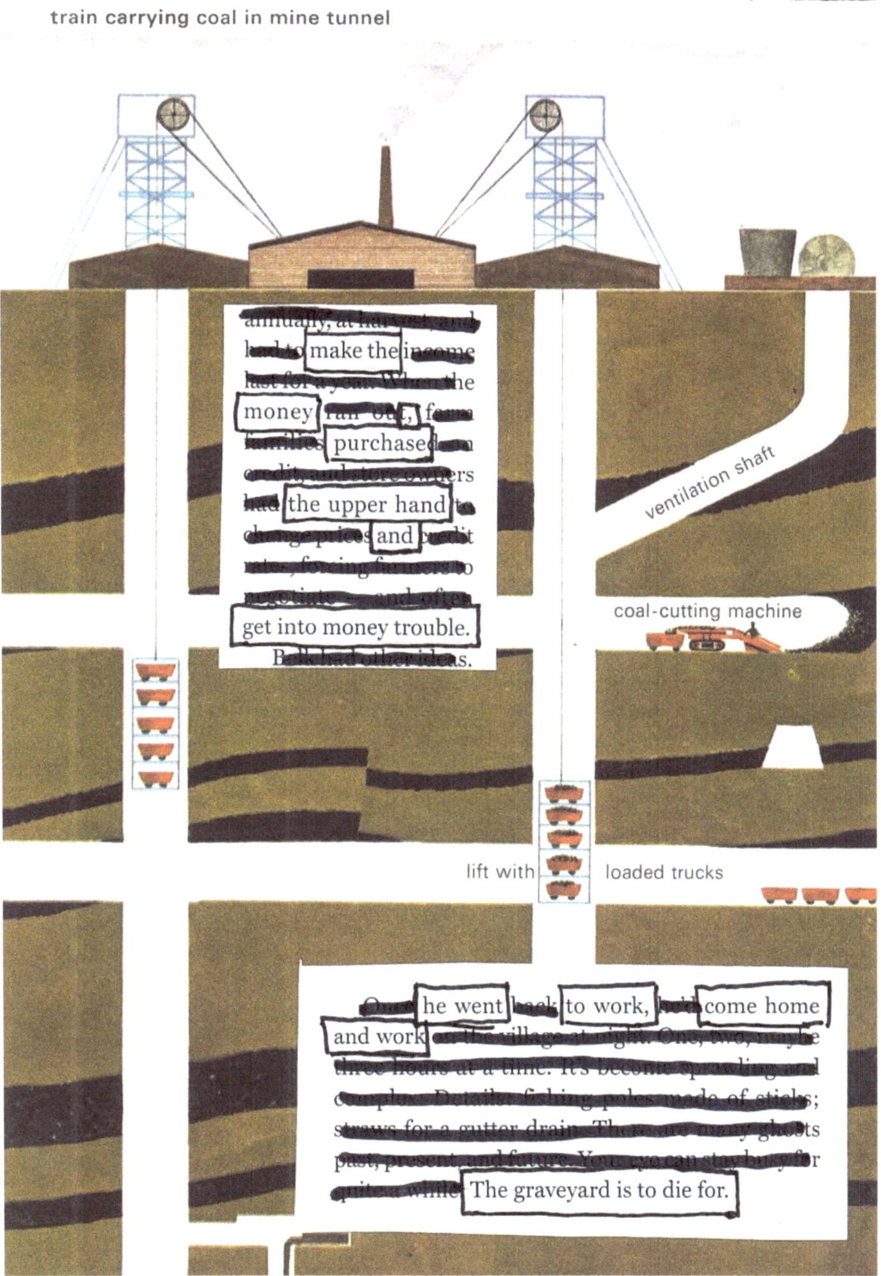

Make the money, purchase the upper hand, and get into money trouble. He went to work, come home and work. The graveyard is to die for.

The family is said to be

a bitter poem.

Their living changes and grows,

but it is too small for his ambition.

Sometimes "It was just a lot of hard work."

"We didn't get to do any of the fun stuff."

"We're putting together adults. They're so hard to find."

It occurs to me that your back end is a tiny town.

The cook chats me up.

I was building a reputation in a household when I started a major transformation. It attracted attention. I led the development of the future.

Stress set up shop, but his wife got fed up, so

he creates a different product.

Shout-out to the scary forever.

Stay married. This is clearly an option

because of their ability to work together, but there are risks.

One spouse could be a worst-case scenario.

Sometimes, something treasured was originally under construction.

Still wanting bigger, better quality, and

grand gestures of love and appreciation.

My husband wished I wanted to make love too.

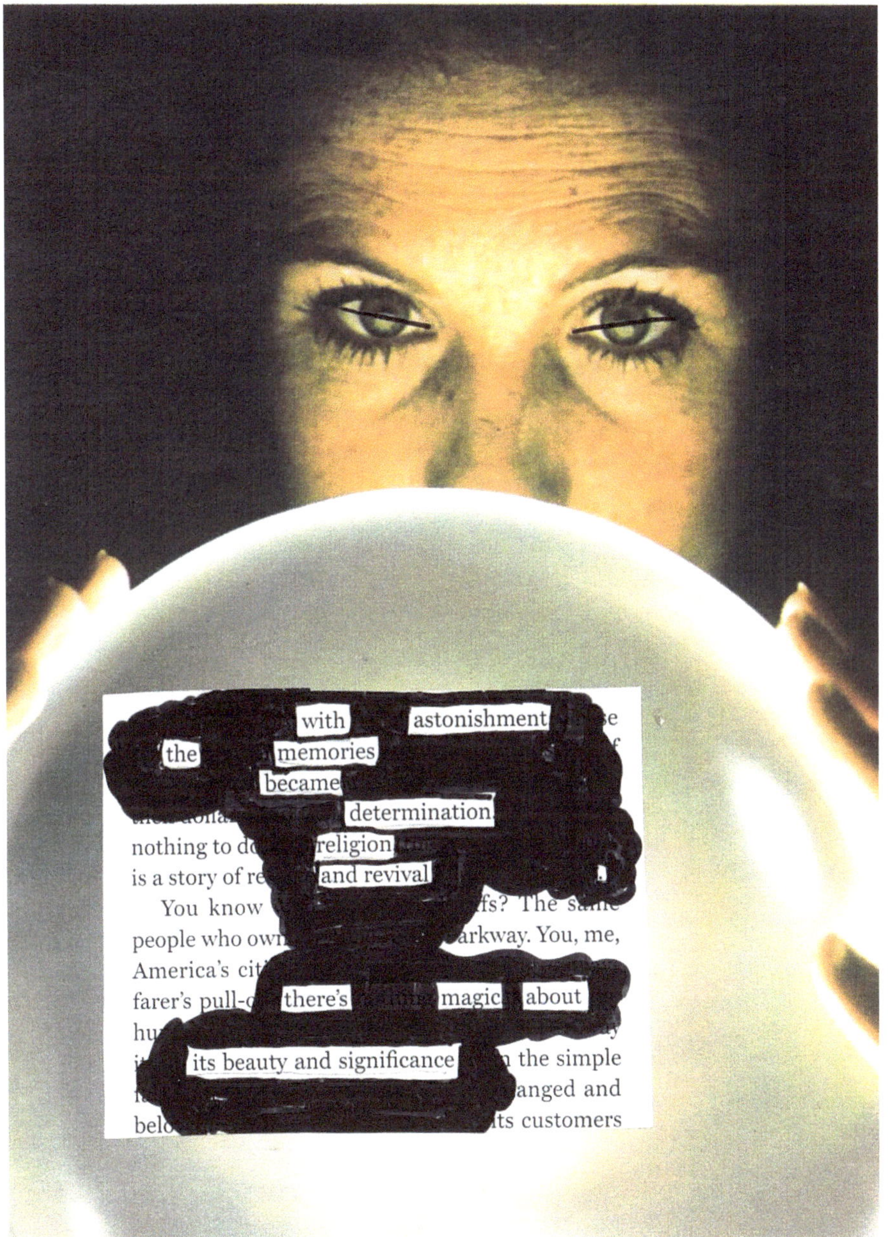

With astonishment the memories became determination, religion, and revival. There's magic about its beauty and significance.

I had to admit the role we play, and yet, we still believe that getting it just right is good for everyone.

We discussed love, raw and real.

In a different light, I saw how human we were.

Most of us, honestly, don't appreciate what it means to envision unison.

I, for one, acknowledge the gentle man.

We eventually come together.

The latest collaboration is poetry.

Its presence, tightly coiled, emerges.

Mature, it deepens, fertile and loose.

The sun illuminates the two,

undulating.

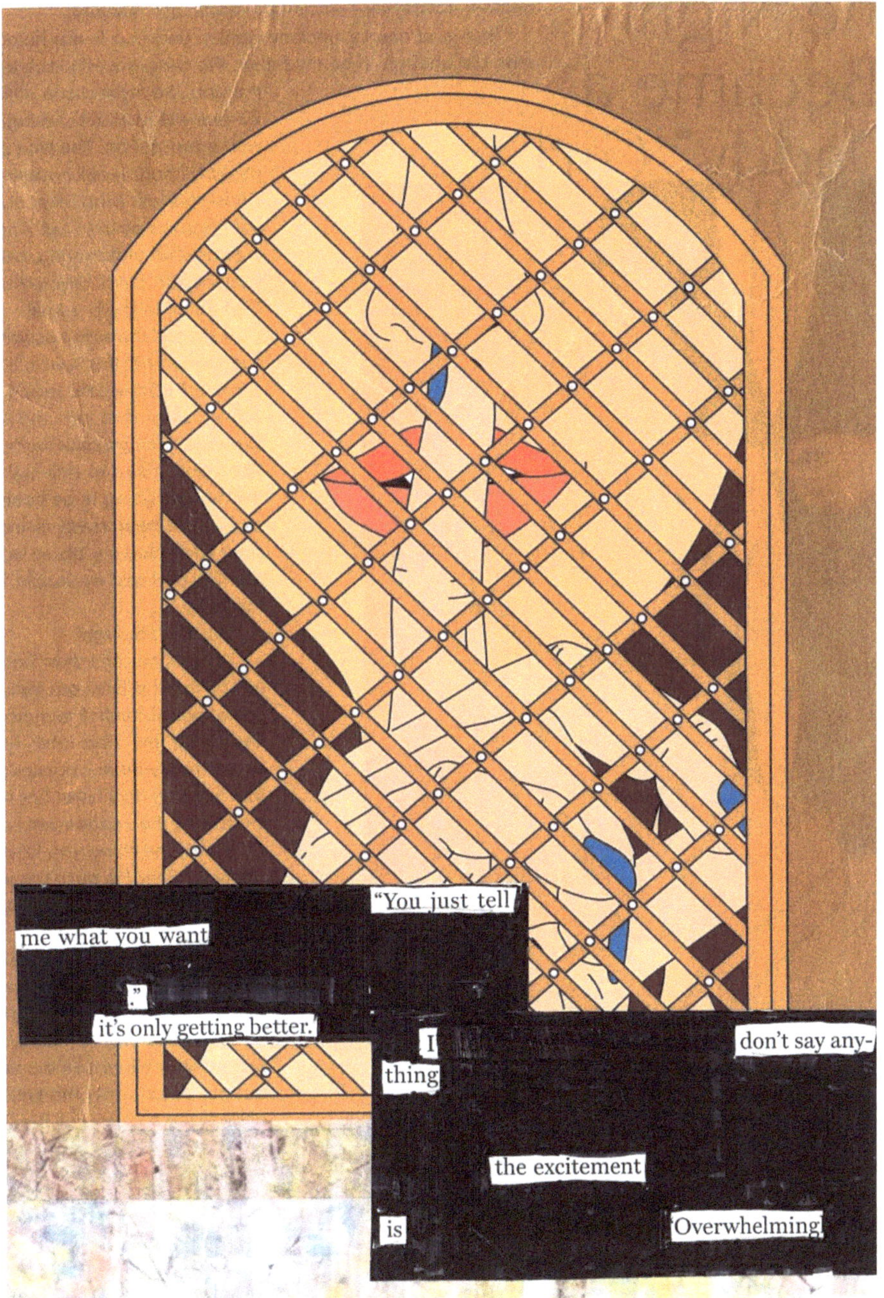

"You just tell me what you want." It's only getting better. I don't say anything. The excitement is overwhelming.

A Homeric back and forth,

the spectacular climax arrives with triumph.

Lovers should be delighted, beautiful, and gorgeous-looking.

The best I'd tasted in years.

See the father trying to be more patient,

a little more willing to show them how to land.

It's always good for kids to see their parents try to learn.

The choice benefits the people you love.

A kind and beautiful man holds knowledge and wisdom.

His work is for generations to come.

His wife and daughter will light candles and revel.

They didn't have much, but they usually had enough.

She held nothing against time, her dignity still very much intact.

She's proud of what's become of her improvements over the years.

"She had an infinite amount of patience and a will to make things happen. She was one of those fearless women who just wouldn't take no for an answer. You can learn a lot from a woman like that." Honor her.

The absolute center of life itself—the family.

This is an opportunity that they worked and loved hard on.

An old favorite can still feel the same.

Forty years rolled into this day, a legacy.

Watch the sunrise, watch an afternoon age into evening.

A gravity all its own.

Build bewilderment. "Every day, all day. On weekends too.

That skill kept me from losing my mind."

The day is theirs again, an ocean of home.

When you find the world a tolerant, generous, loving place, think about patient hands and us—together.

He lovingly referred to his wife.

"I have such fond memories of her."

You can't close the doors to the memories.

He keeps his on display.

It's no small honor to remember.

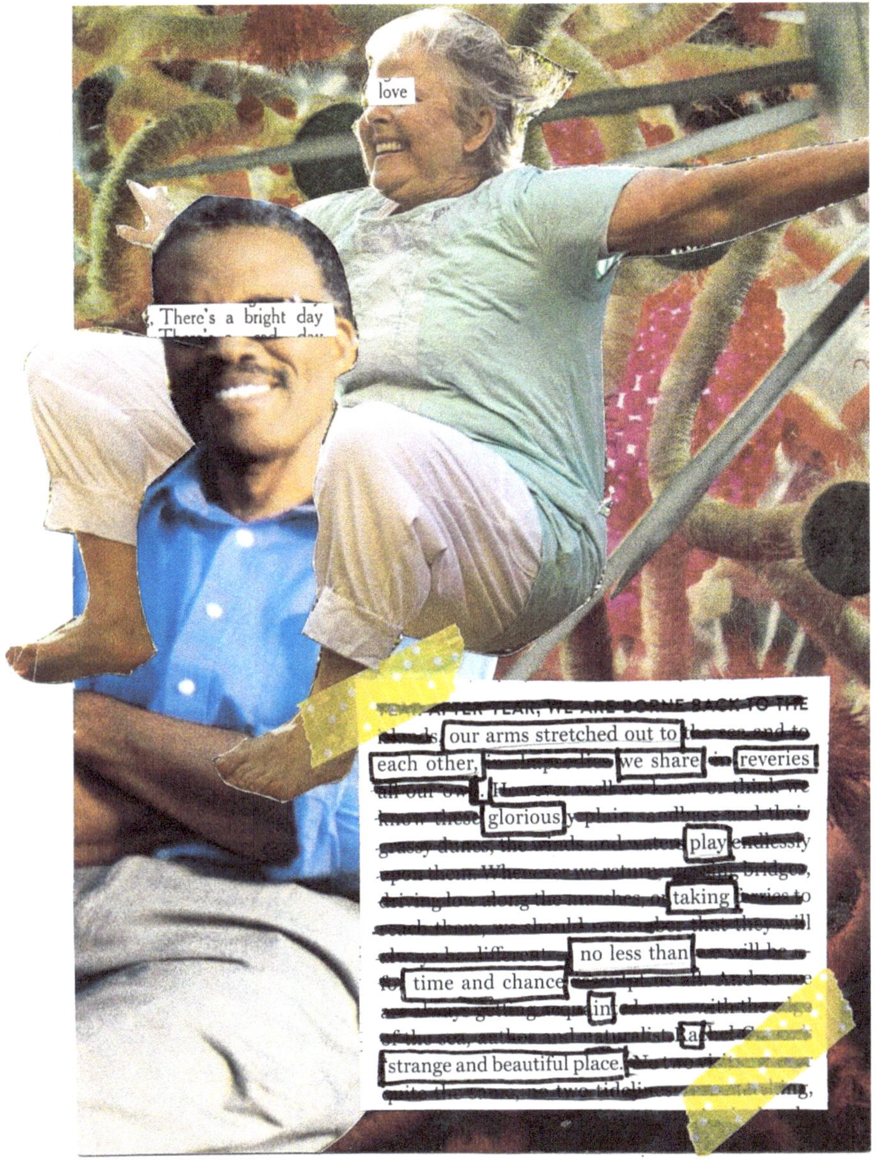

Our arms stretched out to each other, we share reveries.

Glorious play taking no less than time and chance

in a strange and beautiful place.

What a gift of God to have been

given time to be in love.

Acknowledgements

Anyone who has ever published will tell you that releasing a book is akin to giving birth: painful, terrifying, and surprisingly empowering. At least once you get past the labor pains (*Why do I feel like dying?*), post-partum depression (*No one cares, no one likes it. My art is trash and everything is a disaster!*), and the long trek into the new normal (*That wasn't so bad, was it? Maybe I'll do it again!*).

Thankfully, by the time y'all read this, one of the following fantastic friends or family members will have scraped me off the kitchen floor and helped me get back on track after that rough publishing post-partum period.

To my family:

Jared, Jubilee and Rejoice: Life with the three of you is a gift, and I am so grateful for the freedom we have to spend our days working and living and learning and loving alongside each other. It's been a blessing I never saw coming, and somehow that makes it even better.

Mama, Daddy, Pops, and Ma: Y'all's examples of happy 40-plus year marriages are true generational wealth. My girls are too young to understand what a blessing it is, but I am too old *not* to understand. Thank y'all for pointing me and Jared to the One who holds our hearts in His hands.

Katie and Asa, and Fairlight: Thank you both for giving me my niece and for being my friend. I appreciate that especially after I was so mean to you as a child, Kate. Fairlight, I would happily give you a million dollars if I had it. You and those dimples live up to your name.

Ian: I've said it before and I'll say it again. You are a picture of God's grace and His protective hand. I am excited to see what your future holds.

To my friends:

Jess, you have been here since the beginning of this bizarre project, always gassing me up and encouraging me to keep going. Who knew finding those photos that weekend in Ellijay was the start of this project? You are a gift to me. Thank God you are such a weirdo. I love you.

Having been blessed with so many different friend groups, I am truly rich indeed. I would be lost without my Beach Babes, my Tinkergarten Moms, my Trinity Ladies, and my fellow Southern Scribes. A special thank you to Deena and Sherry for listening to my rambling Marco Polos about this publishing journey and unrelated nonsense. Y'all get me.

Abby, thank you for your friendship and for designing this amazing cover! It's rare to find a version of yourself in another person. You've been a wonderful surprise!

There are so many others who have encouraged me along the way, and I'm hesitant to list them for fear of leaving someone out, but please know that if you have ever spoken life into me, I have not forgotten it. Your words are a priceless treasure.

Thank you to everyone who donated their trash to this project and to all those who have attended my workshops. I'm thrilled to help you start hoarding little scraps of paper for your own projects.

Lastly, thank you to God for the gift of this life and all these wonderful people who bring me so much joy. You've cracked my heart wide open, and I hope I never get over it.

I love y'all!

—Tristan

Thank you for reading *Such Fond Memories*!

If you enjoyed it, please consider rating and leaving a review on Amazon and Goodreads. Reviews mean so much to me and other authors. Your feedback is invaluable since it allows the algorithm to show our books to new readers. I would be lost without you and your support. Thank you so much!

Also by Tristan Tuttle

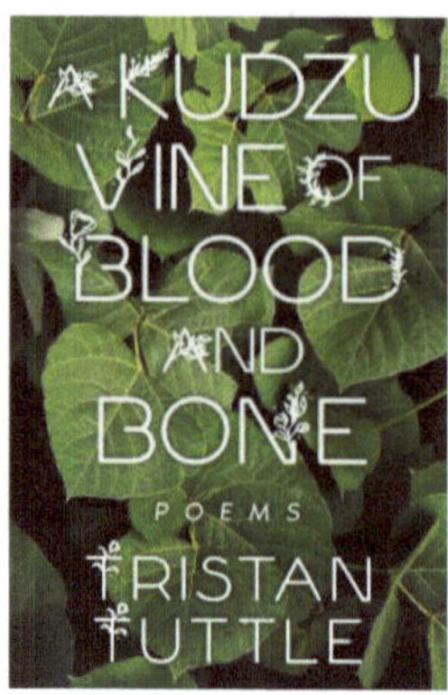

A 2022 #1 New Release on Amazon

A tender and honest debut poetry collection about the intersection of motherhood, nature, and the spirituality that binds it all together.

"Reading this collection feels like a radical form of self-care, like resistance against a world that tells us there's only one right way to exist." —Nykia B.

"[…] it's a beautiful collection of poems about motherhood, the natural world, and a hands-in-the-dirt, clear-eyed kind of faith." —Cat Q.

![stars]

"If you appreciate Kate Baer, but have been wanting a representation of motherhood that is more hopeful, joyful—turn to Tristan Tuttle" —Amy E.

About the Author

Tristan Tuttle is a writer and mixed media artist. She is the founder of the Southern Scribe Society and loves to encourage other writers and artists on their journey. Her poetry collection *A Kudzu Vine of Blood and Bone* was a #1 New Release on Amazon. She teaches art workshops on blackout poetry and collage several times a year. Keep up with her events and adventures at www.tristantuttle.com as well as on Instagram @tristantuttle. You can sign up for her Love Letters on Substack at www.tristantuttlewrites.substack.com.